The Tinsel Tango
A Dickens Holiday Novella
Dance of Love
By
Bonnie Edwards

The Tinsel Tango

Bonnie Edwards

Published by Bonnie Edwards

Copyright 2020 & 2021 Bonnie Edwards

Cover Design: selfpubbookcovers.com/RLSather

A shorter version of The Tinsel Tango was previously published in the anthology Christmas Comes to Dickens.

Table of Contents

This book is dedicated to truth seekers and those who love the spirit of Christmas.

And Ted, always.

The Tinsel Tango by Best Selling Author Bonnie Edwards

THE TANGO AKA THE DANCE of Love...

Brenna James is ordered to take an early Christmas break in Dickens to regroup and relax with family. She chooses tango lessons to take her mind off her pending, desperately wanted, promotion. Her instructor, Jett ... Smith is intriguing and mysterious because Jett may not be who he says he is...

Jett Somers is masquerading as a dance instructor while searching for the inventor of a process that could change the world. Jett's never had a Christmas before, but Brenna sweeps him up in her family and her Christmas spirit.

When his integrity is questioned in a very public way, Jett must race to restore his good name and salvage his relationship with Brenna.

Can one more tango give him everything he longs for?

Chapter One

Brenna James needed to relax, and recharge, and she had to care enough to do it. But she didn't *want* to relax or recharge. She wanted her promotion and relaxing wouldn't get her the Marketing Director position she'd worked hard for. "Arrgh! This is stupid!"

Driving to Dickens alone when she normally crowded into her father's SUV with her mom and sister, felt like spite against her boss.

"See?" she muttered to the empty car, imagining Bry's smug face. "I'm fine. I got myself this far, didn't I?" Her stomach growled from hunger, and she was still two miles out of town, but closing fast.

Over the past months, she'd worked herself down to a too-thin, too-anxious wraith of her former self. She'd given her all and yet, here she was with direct orders from Bry to recharge and regroup because she was too anxious and...

Having panic attacks hadn't helped her either. So, yeah, she needed to find a way to quit freaking out when things at work came at her like belches of burning lava. Gasping for air, clutching her chest, and storming around the room searching for an exit wasn't a good look for her.

When all that had happened in the middle of her career-making presentation before an audience of twelve it had been noticed. Big time. She could still see their expressions of shock, horror, and pity as she'd lost her—shi—control all over the boardroom.

The humiliation made her sour and worse, the kind words from the V.P. of Accounts, Bry Johnson, had been a death knell. The truth was Bry hadn't been smug when he'd talked to her, he'd been concerned. "Take some time off, it's nearly Christmas. Aren't you heading to that town your family drags you to?"

Dickens. Yes, she was heading to Dickens for a James family Christmas. While she was there, Bry had suggested she soak up the small-town ambiance, the quaint atmosphere, the boring, old-fashioned traditions.

Ugh.

She'd have to share a room with her sister, Kayley, and their cousin, Trix. They'd flip a coin for the bunkbeds, or the single bed jammed into the corner of the tiny room. Then they'd flip again for the top or bottom bunk. Secretly, she loved the top bunk and no matter what happened with the coin toss, she offered to take it.

That might be fun. Seeing her family would be cool. She hadn't seen them in far too long. Thanksgiving had come and gone because she'd been grinding the campaign for Cheez-Wackos. She'd worked straight through the holiday on the campaign that should've guaranteed her promotion. Trying to find the words to sell a product full of unpronounceable chemicals as a healthy snack had done her in. Had made her ripe for panic when she'd faced all those bored faces.

They'd hated her concept on sight and when she'd seen their clients fidgeting, panic had come over her like an eruption. She'd dropped the remote control for the large screen from nerveless fingers. All she'd worked for slid away into a drain. The images on the screen had swirled before her. Black spots had narrowed her vision and her lungs had just...stopped. That's when she'd wanted to run, run, run...

If she didn't quit thinking about it, she'd be back there, in that panicked state. She pulled her car to a stop on the gravel shoulder. The sign welcoming her to Dickens had been freshly painted in forest green with gold scroll lettering. Someone had stuck a bright red plastic poinsettia flower on top of the sign.

Christmas had come to Dickens. And so had Brenna James.

The season and all its traditions would help her regain her focus. Then, she could return to work and wow Bry with her can-do attitude.

JETT SOMERS TACKED up a flyer on the bulletin board inside Dorrit's Diner. He'd already put one up in Morty's Deli on the town square. What a place this was. The town of Dickens was quintessential New England. It had a town Common with a gazebo, a statue of some guy who'd founded the place, and what looked to be a closed merry-go-round. Mid-December would be too cold for putting your kids on horses and fairy creatures.

He hoped the girl who'd put up flyers looking for her lost cat, Snowball, had found it. Every pole in the square had a picture and a plea for help. Poor kid.

The diner was in full holiday mode. Shiny red three-dimensional stars hung over the booths. Tinsel streamers crisscrossed the ceiling and fake snow had been sprayed in each corner of the front window. There was more, but Jett tried to ignore the over-the-top clutter.

Since he'd arrived on the first of the month, he'd heard lots of versions of White Christmas. So far, his favorite was from the eighties' rockers, *Doug and the Slugs*.

His flyer secure, he settled at the counter and before he asked, an empty mug sat in front of him.

"Coffee?"

It was the regular afternoon server. Her name tag said she was Laurel, although he'd never used her name. She was there each afternoon, ready with a smile and a mug.

"Coffee." He winked and gave the woman a nod. "Thanks. Best coffee in town."

Laurel poured in a swooping low-high-low motion. "We like to think so." She leaned toward him and in a whisper, gave away the diner's secret ingredient. He raised his eyebrows at the information and mugged a look of shock. She chuckled.

They shared a sense of humor and after a morning working remotely with his assistant, Sophia, he made a point of coming in for coffee every day at this time. People like Laurel on the frontlines were pure gold. They were never paid enough, but they were vital for a business that depended on repeat customers.

Dickens had a lot of gold. Friendly people, with the right amount of easygoing curiosity without being pushy. They seemed genuine and satisfied to believe he'd come to town to give tango lessons to the crowd who holidayed here for Christmas.

He hoped he wouldn't be here long, but it could be fun to be part of a small-town Christmas season. He never had much use for the holiday, having never had a family, but he'd seen a few seconds here and there of movie classics set at this time of year. The season supposedly brought out the best in people.

Jett understood the basics of Christmas. He had Sophia buy gifts people didn't need, treated his employees to bonuses, and gave them paid time off from Christmas Eve to New Year's Day. After he'd done his duty, he'd go somewhere warm with his woman-of-the-month and bury himself in planning the new year.

Spending these weeks in Dickens would be different. He was alone, for one thing. And he planned to enjoy the season, not overwork. Next time he mentored a business and invested, he'd be looking at the people involved, too, not just the bottom line and potential for profit.

Since he'd never had a family, he hadn't understood what could tear one apart. His most recent protégé, Paul Forster still struggled to find his way after losing his wife and children to his fledgling business. Now-familiar regret ran through Jett's gut. Paul's whole reason for starting *Bring the Change* had been to support his family and improve the family lives of thousands of the poor and disenfranchised.

Jett would handle things better this time. He'd be sure not to push too hard or expect more than was humanly possible. Paul had given his all to his business and then lost the wife he loved. Jett had pushed him too hard and neither of them had seen the end coming.

If the business Jett hoped was here showed promise, he'd be extra careful. He'd never again be the instrument of destruction for a family. Never.

Chapter Two

"Aunt Lolly," Brenna said as she took a seat next to a man nursing a mug of coffee in Dorrit's. Her aunt turned toward her immediately, already grinning from ear to ear.

"Brenna! You're early," she leaned across the counter and smooched Brenna on the cheek. "What brings you here already?"

Early? Oh, right. She and the rest of the crew didn't normally arrive until the twentieth or later. Today was only the fifth. Twenty days to Christmas. Twenty-five days to the new year. Plenty of time to get her head straight. She hoped.

"I just wanted extra Christmas time with my favorite aunt," she responded with a grin. Lolly had already slipped a mug in front of her. *She must keep them up her sleeve.*

"Nonsense, you're here so we can fatten you up. I've never seen you this skinny. Have you been eating?" Real concern dripped from Lolly's eyes into Brenna's, making her shift in discomfort.

And it wasn't the first time she'd answered this question lately. "Of course. You know I love to eat." Her stomach growled louder than it had in the car. Half the restaurant must've heard it.

"Hmph," came the reply from Lolly. "I'll get you a muffin right away."

Great, now the family would be stuffing her full. She could taste Gramma's ginger snaps now. Her mouth watered.

The man next to her shifted as he lifted his mug for a sip. The movement caused his scent, spicy and manly, to drift by her nose. His aftershave was both mystery and intrigue. She flashed him a glance.

Great profile. Strong nose and chin, perfect skin. His hair could use a trim, but she liked the slight wave that appeared at his collar. If it were the 1970s, he'd have a head full of wavy, russet-colored hair.

He'd probably pass those red highlights off to his kids. Nice.

Lolly filled her mug, and her glance went from Brenna to the man and back again. Being caught checking out a man brought heat to Brenna's cheeks. Aunt Lolly wasn't the kind to keep her observations to herself, either. She'd tell the whole family that she'd caught Brenna *lookin'*.

"Brenna, meet the new guy in town." Lolly raised her palm to indicate the man should say his name.

"You must be new here, if my aunt doesn't know your name yet."

"Been here a few days. I'm Jett," he said. "Jett...Smith." He turned his face to hers. Warm brown-sugar eyes took her measure.

"I'm Brenna James. I'm here for Christmas," she said. She offered her hand, and he took it in his. One warm shake and she felt it right up her arm and into her chest.

"But, sweetie, you never come this early," Lolly interjected. "What's going on?"

"I'll explain later," she replied with a significant look to her left. Jett Smith didn't need to know her business. Although she'd kind of like to know his.

"I'm finished here," he said pleasantly. "Have your reunion in peace." With that, he slapped a couple of bills on the counter and left without a backward glance.

She got it. If she were the one leaving, she wouldn't look back at him, either. *Liar.* That man was worth more than a second glance, but she schooled her features into indifference and shrugged.

"Amy, family's here," Lolly called through to the kitchen. "I'm taking a break."

Inwardly, Brenna sighed. Coming to Dorrit's first had been a tactical error, but she'd needed coffee and a friendly face. Not to mention a snack.

"Fine with me," came Amy's faint reply.

With that, Brenna picked up her coffee mug and headed to a booth for a chat. If she'd been smarter, she'd have stopped by during the lunch rush. Lolly would've been too busy to grill her about her early arrival. But now with most of the customers fed or gone, Lolly would be all over her.

"It's nothing big," Brenna said to forestall more questions as her aunt, plated muffin in hand, slid in across from her. "I need a bit of R and R. I've been working a lot of hours lately."

"Uh huh?" Lolly looked skeptical and knit her fingers together in expectation of a full confession. Family, they could read her like a book.

"And a window opened up for me where I could take extra time off. Where better to come than Dickens in December?"

"Uh huh."

Brenna set her lips in a line. "That's it, that's all."

"Uh huh."

"What's new with you?" She tossed out. "How's Trix?"

A look of indecision crossed Lolly's usually content features. She glanced heavenward as if for strength. "Her moron of a husband is leaving her."

"Oh, no!" Her cousin, her dear, sweet, trusting cousin Trix had been abandoned. Never mind Trix's husband was a snake. Her cousin had been blind to his faults. "How is she?"

"Honestly? I'm not sure. Sometimes, I hear bitterness in her voice. Then, it's gone, like smoke."

"When is she arriving?" Although Trix grew up here, she spent the Christmas season at Gramma's house with the rest of the family so "all the kids" could be together. "All the kids" were now in their early- to mid-thirties. But still, tradition was important in Dickens. Trix's husband, Dale, had usually sacked out on the sofa.

"She'll be here on the twentieth, like usual." Lolly unclasped her hands and then knit them again. She was nervous. That reading-like-a-book thing went both ways.

Brenna leaned in. "What?" she said in a low voice.

"That rotter got another woman pregnant and dumped Trix like trash."

Brenna had never heard such venom in her aunt's voice. Lolly's hurt for her daughter sat in her eyes.

Tears smarted in response to her aunt and cousin's pain. Trix had wanted a baby for years. She'd confessed last Christmas that she was asking her husband about medical procedures, but he'd said they couldn't afford it.

"I can understand why she'd feel bitter." Her heart broke for Trix. "When did this all happen?"

"Two days ago."

"I'm sorry, I wasn't aware." She'd been ducking calls from the family ever since her panic attacks had begun last month. And when Bry had told her to take time off last week, she'd ghosted most people in her life. Popping up here out of the blue must seem strange, but with Trix's news, no one would look too closely at Brenna.

"No, don't worry about not knowing. Trix wants to tell Gramma in person, so we've kept it quiet."

"All right, I can keep a secret."

Sometimes family needed back up and Brenna would have Trix's back on this.

JETT HAD A FOUR O'CLOCK lesson with a recent widow looking for a new challenge. She was one of the holiday visitors and had explained she needed the distraction. The owner, Mrs. Moore, was on the phone when he arrived ten minutes ahead of the appointed time. She'd called her dance school, Tiny Tim's School of Dance because as a child she'd worn braces. He loved the hook inherent in the name.

Who wouldn't take a second glance at a business that seemed like an oxymoron or at the least, ironic? Anyone looking at the sign or the website would be hooked into reading more. Great marketing appealed to him.

Mrs. Moore was clever and kind and not concerned with why he'd come to Dickens, because as she put it, "People come and go here. You either love this place and atmosphere or you don't." He hadn't asked if he looked like a man who'd stay because he wasn't. He never stayed long anywhere.

Like the rest of Dickens, the studio was in full Christmas season dress. A phony tree stood in the corner, full of ornaments and tinsel garlands. If his nose was telling him the truth, Mrs. Moore had scented the air with pine today.

Sometimes the studio smelled of ginger and cinnamon.

"Are your lessons going well?" Mrs. Moore asked after she'd hung up, looking pleased and secretive. Something sly and mischievous glided through her gaze.

"My flyers keep disappearing and people call because they've taken them home or to their hotel. When they read that my lessons are private and only available until the new year, they panic and don't want anyone else to get in." Which was fine if he really was a dance instructor.

"Maybe you should stay in Dickens longer."

He scrubbed his hand down his face. "It is nice here," he conceded. A sound from the doorway made him turn. The widow had arrived.

She was the second most spectacular woman he'd seen today. She walked in, stuck both arms up in the air and announced, "Call me Marva!"

Marva was dressed in purple and orange. The color choice flowed into her brilliantly dyed hair. She wore a sparkly pair of dance shoes, purple tights, and a sequined orange dress that ended far above her dimpled knees. Marva twirled and removed her purple velvet cape as she moved.

She was a treasure and he loved her on sight.

Mrs. Moore raised her eyebrows and with a nod to the marvelous Marva, scurried out the door.

Jett greeted his student, had her sign her waiver in case of injury, and walked around her to check her posture. She needed help. A lot of help.

He touched her on the back of her shoulders, prodding her to straighten. "Use your core."

"Honey, do you really believe there's a core under this belly?"

He leaned in next to her ear. "Sweetie, of course there is. And by the time this lesson is over, yours will be screaming."

She gave a visible shudder and laughed. But she was game and challenged him to make her hurt.

Still, Marva only came in second in the stunning-woman-met-today contest. First place went to Brenna. Up close he'd got caught in her beautiful green eyes, saw her smattering of freckles and her long black lashes. The touch of her hand had sent a thrill straight down. The subtlety of her beauty had slammed him stupid and all he'd been able to do was run out of Dorrit's like a bumbling kid.

Chapter Three

Jett worked poor Marva hard and by the end of the hour she glistened with her effort and her lipstick had been chewed off. Her palms sat weightily on his shoulders. "Honey," she said through a heavy breath, "do you believe I can do this?"

"I believe." And he did. "You're lighter on your feet than you realize."

"Charmer," she declared. "I think I found my core." She bent over, put her hands on her knees, and groaned. "I need a hot Epsom salts bath."

He showed her a couple of stretches to try at home and then he settled her cape around her shoulders. "Don't forget to soak your feet, too. They're not new shoes, are they?"

"Yes, but I walked around inside my rental in them as soon as I signed up for lessons. They should be broken in."

"Smart." He gave her a smile. "Remember your posture at all times. You can train yourself to stand up straighter." He showed her how to pin her shoulders back against the wall.

"I'll try," she promised. "Will you be at the tree lighting ceremony?"

"Unlikely."

"The locals tell me it's the biggest event of the season."

"Bigger than Christmas Day?"

"Honey, there are no available men wandering the streets on the twenty-fifth. But I could get lucky at the ceremony," she said with a chuckle. "It would be nice to see your smiling face. You're the first person to say more than 'good day' to me."

He chuckled. Marva was something. "Good luck, then," he said cheerily. "The single men in this town will fall at your feet."

And he wondered where he'd be on the twenty-fifth. Like Marva, he'd taken a short-term rental rather than a hotel, so he wasn't sure if he'd get Christmas dinner. Maybe he could order in.

His next student arrived, and Marva hobbled out, shouting back a promise to return.

GRAMMA RETURNED HOME shortly after four and Brenna climbed out of her car to greet her. The older woman covered her mouth in surprise and then opened her car door.

"Brenna, my dear! I'm thrilled to see you." They hugged and Gramma tugged her toward the veranda steps. "Even as thin as you are."

Brenna pulled to a stop. "Gramma, I came early," she said. She hadn't been considerate of her grandmother's schedule. "I hope that's okay that I did. I don't want to impose."

"Impose? Of course not. Come in, come in. I was worried that horrid job would keep you in New York again, the way it did for Thanksgiving. Your mother was fit to be tied." And she pulled Brenna along again.

"She never said anything." But that was her mother's way. Whatever her daughters threw at her, she accepted. Clearly, her mom couldn't hide her disappointment from her own mother and Gramma made sure Brenna knew it. A stab of guilt made her inwardly wince. "I didn't mean to hurt her, Gramma. I put the job—my career, I mean—before my family. I shouldn't have."

"I'm not the one you need to tell." She busied herself unlocking the front door.

"I'll apologize when I see her, don't worry." The apology would be expected in person, not via text.

Her grandmother opened the ornate, original front door of the huge Victorian house. She'd lived here for her whole adult life. The oval window held a wreath of holly and twinkling lights. Gramma pointed at it. "This is new," she said to change the subject to small talk, for which Brenna was grateful.

Her grandmother wasn't one to harp on things. She'd let Brenna know her absence at Thanksgiving had been hard and now it was on Brenna to soothe the hurt feelings. And she would. When her mother arrived, Brenna planned to have a long heart-to-heart to explain her decision to work over the last holiday.

Following Gramma's lead, Brenna walked through the gaily decorated house and exclaimed over the new pieces. Gramma liked to rotate her garlands and where she put her Victorian Christmas village. This time it was on an antique table near the fireplace.

Brenna felt bad about keeping Trix's secret, but divorce was another thing better discussed in person, especially since Trix had been betrayed on so many levels. After the announcement was made the flock of James women would encircle Trix with love and support. And a good deal of wine.

Brenna helped her Gramma raid the fridge for leftovers, and settled in for a comfy, casual dinner. The conversation flowed around the family and then to the new happenings in Dickens.

"How's business? Slowing down? Or are you as busy as ever?" Brenna asked.

Gramma smiled winsomely. "I've rented out some hours when I'm not teaching."

"You haven't done that before. Who's rented the time?"

Gramma stood and collected her plate. As she turned away toward the large original porcelain sink, she said, "His name is Jett and he's teaching the tango. Fun, right? These days dance is all about salsa, but there's something alluring about the tango." She faced Brenna again and waved her hand in front of her face. "The tango is H-O-T hot. And Jett is startlingly handsome."

"Is he?" But Brenna had felt the sweep of heat just from the man's glance. The scent of his aftershave was stamped into her memory. It had to be the same man. How many Jetts could there be in a town the size of Dickens?

"To be held by a man like that. It's every woman's dream," her grandmother murmured. "Oh, don't look at me like that. I'm seventy but I'm not dead yet. Any woman would look twice at him." She cocked an eyebrow.

Oh, no, that look was always followed by a mischievous suggestion. "Whatever you're cooking up? No. You will not set me up with a man who's only been here a few days."

Gramma folded her arms across her middle. "Now, how do you know that my darling granddaughter?"

Caught. "I may have stopped by Dorrit's and inadvertently sat beside him at the counter where Aunt Lolly introduced us." She hadn't meant to sit right there, but it was the closest stool to where her aunt was standing at the time. That's all. Of course, she hadn't noticed Jett's broad shoulders and tapered waist and gorgeous hair the moment she stepped inside the diner. Suspicion curled through Brenna. "But my own aunt, a woman I love and trust, didn't mention he was renting studio time from my grandmother. Why is that?"

Gramma had the grace to flush. "You've been working too hard, and Jett seems like such a good guy. What's the harm in you signing up for tango lessons? He's got an eight-lesson bundle and it'll be good for you."

Gramma had embraced dance as a child when her braces had come off her legs. She felt the discipline and athleticism had helped her regain her childhood and her life. Everyone she met had been told her story and no doubt Jett had been told, too.

"Aunt Lolly sure got on the phone quickly after I left the diner." She narrowed her eyes. It was a five minute drive.

Gramma shifted a shoulder to indicate Brenna had got it right.

"Lolly called you and told you I'd met Jett while you were still at the studio?"

"Sort of."

Gramma had put on a good act of looking surprised when she'd found Brenna in the driveway. "What else did Lolly tell you?"

"You look tired and stressed and that's the truth. You do. And you've lost weight."

"I shouldn't have come here," Brenna muttered.

"Oh, honey, of course you should have. Dickens is a healing kind of place, especially at Christmas. Your heart told you to come. You need to suck up the good vibes, set your troubles aside, and relax into the season." Gramma moved closer and Brenna rose to be pulled into a hug. "When you go back to your life, you'll feel stronger and ready to take on the world again."

"You think?" Her voice went soft and childlike, and Brenna accepted that there was no place like *this* place and no family as warm and loving as hers. Jett's scent prickled her nose again, like a sensual memory. "Maybe tango lessons would be fun. And I could use the refresher. It's been years since you taught me." She nodded. "I have to fill my days with something before everybody arrives."

"That's my girl," Gramma comforted.

"I'll call him to book my lessons. How many people per class?"

"Jett's offering one-on-one. You'll be all alone with him. Doing the tango."

Chapter Four

Billie Adamson had stumbled on a revolutionary method of prolonging battery life that would change the world. Jett wanted to be the man who brought the process to light. He'd seen his first clue in an online chat room dedicated to science. A comment here and there had added to the story and as far as Jett knew he was the only one in the business world to pick up on it. He'd joined the conversation, as he sometimes did, to pull out more pieces of information until he was certain this Billie was onto something big.

He doubted, from Billie's answers, that the young man understood how big this could be. The applications around the world would change everything from heavy metal mining to how far an electric vehicle could drive without recharging. Handheld devices could go twice as long without being plugged in.

He'd moved their conversation to private and then *poof!* Billie had disappeared. He had enough information to figure that the young man lived in or near Dickens.

After a morning spent working remotely, Jett did his usual patrol of the town square, replacing flyers that had wilted or disappeared. The leaves on the huge maples had turned to hues only God could paint, and they skittered in front of him with each footfall. A memory tugged at him from his childhood. A rare, good day as he recalled. His foster parents had taken the whole brood of kids to a park for an event, and they'd all run wild in the fallen leaves, screeching, and playing.

Mostly, he'd done okay in foster care, but in the end couldn't wait to age out and move ahead. Ahead and away from anything to do with families. They were noisy, messy, and sapped your energy. At least, that's what he'd thought at the time.

But now? Now he looked around Dickens and saw fathers with kids on their shoulders, mothers wiping chins and cooing into strollers, tucking blankets when the wind kicked up. These folks cared and took care and provided their children with love and comfort.

He'd never noticed before how some families worked. In New York and other places, he'd been too busy to look around. And Manhattan wasn't exactly full of these types of families. Not that he'd seen, anyway.

He swung in for his usual mug of coffee from Laurel at Dorrit's, but she wasn't in today. Disappointment wafted through him because he'd hoped to get information on her niece, Brenna. Maybe he'd be lucky enough to see her again.

Stupid idea. He was only here for a handful of weeks. Odd that he'd hope for another chance encounter with a woman he'd shared one glance with. Normally, he went into hot pursuit immediately. His lifestyle didn't allow for wasting time when he saw a woman he wanted.

Last week, before Dickens, he'd have slipped her his card, touched her hand, then a strand of her hair and make a date to see her again. All within minutes.

He'd have been assertive, calm, and deliberate, making no bones about what he wanted. The type of women he found were happy enough to hang out with him for a few weeks before he moved onto another city, another country, another woman.

And at Christmas, he'd find one who wanted to hit a beach and enjoy whatever diamonds he bought for her while he worked.

He wandered over to the studio to chat with Mrs. Moore and see if anyone had walked in through the day to sign up for tango lessons. Odd, but there were still some people who wanted to do things face to face rather than on his hastily constructed website or by email.

But the person he saw inside the studio waiting, wasn't Mrs. Moore, but Brenna James, the most spectacular woman he'd met the day before. *Sorry, Marva.*

"Hi," he said, as he cleared his throat. *Unbelievably urbane.*

"Hello. My grandmother suggested I stop in and book some lessons with you," she said as she walked toward him. "You're teaching the tango?"

She was lovely today; more beautiful than his fevered dreams had made her. Her black hair was up in a ponytail and her green eyes danced with mischief. Dressed in a silk blouse the color of peacock wings, Brenna moved like a dancer, smooth and lithe and...sensual. She'd be an excellent student.

"Your grandmother is Mrs. Moore?"

"Yes," she said through an affectionate smile. "She just left to run errands."

"And Laurel from Dorrit's is your aunt?"

"Yes." She drew out the word as if he were a bright boy for seeing that one plus one equaled two. "They're mother and daughter."

Family. They were all family. He'd fallen into a family full of funny, lovely, smart, women.

"Cool," he said. "She's left for the day?"

Brenna drew to a halt in front of him; so close he could see her freckles again. He drew in a breath and held it.

"Why? Are you afraid to be alone with me? I assure you, I'm perfectly safe." Normally, he played pursuer, but this could be fun. He smiled into her eyes.

"Safe?" he murmured. "I doubt that." Brenna James could be the most dangerous woman on the planet. But just to him. And he didn't care what kind of ride he was in for.

He was in and that was what mattered.

"As it happens, I have a free hour right now."

"Me, too."

He hadn't noticed before, but she'd already hung her coat, scarf, and purse up on one of the hooks provided for students. Her boots, tall and dark red, leaned against the wall. She wore well-worn dance shoes.

"I take it you've had lessons before?"

"Gramma taught all of us to dance as children. She wanted to instill confidence and discipline."

"I see your dance experience in your walk. You move beautifully."

"That's a lovely thing to say," she murmured and licked her lower lip.

He only hoped he could get through this next hour without embarrassing himself. Taking her into his arms seemed like tempting fate...and biology. What was he, fourteen again?

BRENNA FELT LIKE AN untried teenager as she stared up into Jett's handsome face. He took her breath away and she prayed she could make it through the lesson without fainting from lack of oxygen. Yes, the man was that potent. "It's been years since I've danced with a partner. Today couples' dances are reserved for weddings, and even then, it's bride and groom or father and daughter."

"Tango is not a waltz. It's called the dance of love in Argentina." Had his voice lowered an octave? His gaze swept her from head to foot and her body leaned closer of its own volition. "But we'll start with American tango. It's less suggestive."

"Suggestive?" she squeaked. Of course, she knew what he meant but putting the word out there made the moment alive with possibility. She flushed and inwardly cursed her fair complexion.

"You'll see." He walked around her, his shoulder brushing her lightly as he moved. She straightened away from him instinctively, her years on public transit coming back to her when personal space was at a premium. "Yes, you need to be board straight." He spoke into her ear, sending curls of heat down her body to her toes. "But you already know that."

She shivered in reaction.

"Cold?" he asked as he faced her again.

"Not cold, no."

"I think you'll be a perceptive student," he said on a husky note.

"Perceptive?"

"Instinctive, if you prefer." The gleam in his eyes told her he teased, and she flushed harder. He knew the effect he had on her. "I'm going to touch you now, Brenna. Are you ready?"

"Yes, I'm ready." He was a lit match and she the kindling.

And when he held her, she went up in flames.

Chapter Five

Jett lifted Brenna's hand to his shoulder and settled her fingers to lightly cup him there. Her other hand came up and he clasped it. The spark that ran through him at her touch startled, then pleased him. He drew her infinitesimally closer, and she came, allowing the nearness. He didn't know why he noticed every breath, every fluid inch of her, but he did. He'd held countless women this way and none of them had had this effect.

"We begin," he said as he watched her green-eyed gaze widen. She straightened and squared her shoulders perfectly. He slid his left foot toward her. Immediately, she responded by stepping back in time. "Slow, slow, quick, quick, slow," he said with a sidestep at the end. "Good, really good."

She followed his every move smoothly, watching his eyes. Her pupils slowly dilated and he certain his had, too. "Here, we side drag so your knees end up touching, but your feet do not."

Her leg moved. Perfect. Brenna was perfect. "Are you sure you haven't learned this before?"

"We learned waltzes and the rumba. Tap or ballet if we preferred. Gram didn't push us."

He still held her, his hand on her back, his right leg between hers. They'd taken the position naturally. "And you learned to tango," he said, suspicion rising. "Why come here pretending to want lessons?"

She bit her lip, and the adorable action drew his gaze. "I thought I'd got rusty and, to be honest—I can be honest—right?"

"Of course."

Her green eyes glowed with mischief. "My family's driving me batty. Between Aunt Lolly and my grandmother, they're hounding me about why I'm in Dickens this early. I don't want to share my reasons. Not yet."

"A broken heart?" He wasn't sure he wanted to know, but he needed her to be single, broken heart or not. And he had no idea what this had to do with lying about tango lessons.

"No, nothing like that."

He examined her more closely. She had faded smudges under her beautiful eyes, and she might be thinner than most women with her height and build. In fact, he recalled Laurel saying as much in the diner. "Stressed out?" he guessed.

"Apparently. My boss told me I needed some R and R." She shrugged. "I've been super busy at work, and things slow down at this time of year." She batted her eyelashes and frowned. "Anyway, here I am, resting and relaxing."

"Tango will help with that." He understood now. Tango demanded focus and attention to the body. The deep focus the dance demanded could help clear the mind. "What do you do for work?"

"I'm an advertising copywriter," she said. Her gaze sharpened and she backed away.

He had to let her go.

More's the pity. He'd been battling an urge to draw her in for a kiss, but now the moment had passed.

"Long hours?" he asked and then followed immediately with, "And creatively draining."

"Yes, to both." She walked away and he enjoyed the view of her smooth, elegant gait. Taking her coat off the hook she turned back and smiled at him. "Are you going to the tree lighting?"

"If you are," he said making no bones about his interest. Time was short and he suddenly wanted not to be alone over Christmas.

"I'll meet you there," she said. Not a question.

After she walked out without looking back, he pondered their conversation. It didn't seem that Brenna had been entirely truthful. The weeks running up toward year-end were often busier in business than usual. People were in a rush to complete projects and clear their desks when the new year loomed. Procrastinators hell, he liked to call it. He figured advertising had to be the same. Clients pushing for new ad copy for spring would up the stress level in the trenches at ad agencies.

It was curious, of course, but he didn't know her. If she wanted to keep her reason for taking these weeks off a secret that was fine with him.

Still, he wanted to understand her. He'd never been particularly curious about what made a woman tick before. He'd asked no more than the basics. But Brenna pulled at him, and he accepted the pull.

Brenna was gorgeous, at least to him. She was clever and had to be creative if she wrote ad copy. You had to be smart and witty to do that and succeed. You also needed a strong work ethic and the ability to focus and be open creatively at the same time.

Marva arrived in all her wild glory, and he grinned at her appearance. She winced with each step, but her look of fortitude made him proud. "You're hurting," he said.

"Only when I move," she quipped. "But I'm here and I'm determined to do this."

"Have you considered finding a good massage therapist?"

"You read my mind," she said while she hung up her cape. "I've booked a massage right after this. I felt lucky to get in on short notice."

He walked over to her and drew her away from the coat rack area toward the wall of mirrors. "We begin," he said. She huffed out a breath in response.

"Okay. Even my arms hurt," she whined as she lifted them, and he engaged. But she did much better than he'd expected.

When Marva's hour ended, he clapped for her. "I have to say, you've done well."

"Considering I can barely stand up straight."

"You're hard on yourself." His mind moved to his previous student and how gracefully Brenna had moved with him. "You mentioned the tree lighting ceremony yesterday. What time is it?"

"Seven p.m. Are you going after all?"

BRENNA HAD FORGOTTEN to pay for her lessons. Once Jett had taken her in his arms, her mind had scrambled. When their hour was up, she'd bolted and yanked on her coat and boots and then scurried out like a frightened mouse. She'd dashed for home. Only then did she realize she hadn't paid him.

Ridiculous. Where was the confident young woman who'd bulldozed her way to the front of the line for the promotion?

His powerful sensual pull frightened and excited her. *Get a grip*! A smart, sexy man was pursuing her right under the noses of her grandmother and her aunt. Sure, her feelings were juvenile about her elders seeing her in full flirtation mode. But she was no longer the awkward teenage girl that found boys intimidating.

To make her point, if only to herself, she called him and left a voice mail about meeting up at the merry-go-round in the square. "We can get a hot chocolate and take a stroll around the square," she suggested after she'd set the time for an hour before the lighting. "I hope to see you there," she ended.

Dancing with Jett Smith had been the most fun she'd had in far too long. Her shoulders, back and arms felt tight where she'd used muscles that she'd let go soft. A hot soak before meeting Jett would help.

"Wait for me and I'll come with you. We can park at Lolly's," Gramma said when Brenna descended the stairs. She put on her coat, boots, and red-and-white-striped scarf. The scarf was ancient but a must in Dickens in December. Especially for the ceremony. She smiled just draping it around her neck. "Sorry, Gramma, I'm walking over."

"Really? Are you meeting someone?"

"Yes." She refrained from rolling her eyes. "I invited Jett to come along."

The smile that stretched her grandmother's mouth went wide and her cheeks showed every laugh line she'd earned. The expression in her green eyes warmed Brenna.

"Don't wait up," she said, hoping the night might bring more than a simple stroll and hot drink.

True to his word, Jett stood on the far side of the merry-go-round, beside a dark pine that towered over him. He wore a long dark wool coat, a jaunty red scarf and earmuffs that looked like...candy canes? He saw her as she rounded the structure and grinned shyly as if he hadn't believed she'd be here.

The air felt brisk with the promise of winter, and Jett's nose looked red from the chill. Definitely a hot chocolate kind of night.

"Look what I found," he said, holding up a pair of earmuffs. "I got you a set, too." His grin widened and she saw a little boy peeking out from his gaze. Her heart melted and she wondered if he realized how eager and guileless he looked.

"How sweet. I love them," she said as she lifted her lips to his cheek. "Thank you."

She hadn't meant to invite more, but Jett clasped her shoulders and moved the kiss to her mouth. She responded like a starving woman. Maybe she was. She'd certainly been lonely these last months. Maybe a year. *Oh, had it been that long?*

His lips were chilled, but they tasted of peppermint and warmed quickly as she tipped her tongue out to meet his. "I want to kiss you too much to continue here," Jett said in a throaty voice.

She felt the same way, but the good citizens of Dickens were arriving in family groups, and she didn't want to create a spectacle. Everyone here knew Lolly and Gramma and she didn't want, or need, the gossip. Spending the next weeks talking about her and Jett would take all the fun out of it. She was here to regroup so she could return to work ready to step into her promotion at full throttle.

With a satisfied grin firmly in place, Jett set her gift on her head. She adjusted the earmuffs and smiled up at him.

The look he gave her steamed up her spine and she was immediately pulled back to the way he'd held her while they'd danced.

She could be in trouble here. Big trouble. "We're parting ways after Christmas," she said. "Let's keep this light."

"Agreed. But for now, we have weeks ahead of us and anything can happen."

She wondered if his words masked a wish for more or a warning not to hope for more. He draped his arm across her shoulders and snugged her into his side. "I'm so happy," he said. "I've never seen anything like this. All these people coming just to see some lights?"

"Dickens is all about Christmas. The cheer, the decorations, the family time. It's full of wonderful family memories for me."

"Nice," he said quietly.

She tilted her face up. He looked far away. Maybe his memories of the season weren't as special as hers. "Did you have a happy childhood?"

"I got through. I couldn't wait for it to be over. I wanted to be in charge of my life."

Some kids didn't grow up in the happiest of circumstances, so she decided not to pry. If Jett wanted to share more about his young life, he would. But she did have one question.

"How did you become a dance instructor?"

He came back to her, setting aside his darker thoughts. "Dancing put me through high school and college. I grew up watching the kids on the street dancing alone and in teams, but I'd seen a few old movies where couples moved together. I loved how fluid they were, how the steps carried them across the floor. The synchronicity of the couple touched me in ways I didn't understand. I walked into a ballet school and asked if I could learn to be Gene Kelly and Fred Astaire if I took out the trash and swept up."

"Enterprising," she said with a nod. She took his hand and led him toward the coffee shop on the square. Outside stood a lineup of people waiting to get hot drinks from the large urns on a table. "Did you take ballet?"

"No, the manager sent me to a friend of hers who taught me in her home. When I came of age, I moved in there and continued with my education. Without Delia, I wouldn't be who I am today." He frowned.

Which begged the question about who Jett really was? Teaching the tango in a rented studio wouldn't pay the bills. And certainly, wouldn't pay for the beautiful wool coat he wore.

"Are you two still close?"

He shook his head. "She passed away while I was in college. When we met, she was heading for seventy-five and having me in the house gave her purpose, she said. She was a real character. Loud, brash, glorious in her day. Every morning I'd head out with a red smear of lipstick on my cheek."

"She sounds wonderful."

They edged up toward the table and she saw her aunt and grandmother across the square. "Don't look now, but we're about to be accosted."

Of course, he looked around. When he saw the women, he raised his hand and waved. They waved back and immediately put their heads together, like birds on a wire.

"I can only imagine the grilling I'll get when I get home."

He chuckled. "You don't like your family?"

"I love them, but they want things for me I doubt I'll have time for."

"Like?"

She sighed and let go of a dream. "Children, mostly. People who work sixty to seventy hours a week should not be parents." Even off the clock she had to think of her project, whatever it was. Inspiration didn't strike from nowhere. She earned it.

"I've never considered having children," he said. "No time."

"That's sad," she said.

"Yes, it is." He gave her an ironic look she chose to ignore.

"You'd make a fun dad. Buying candy cane earmuffs, dancing the tango."

"Are you saying you wouldn't be a good mother and that makes it okay to work your life away?" He pressed his lips together. "Because work should not define a person. Ambition should not steal away families. They're too hard to come by."

Chapter Six

Jett and Brenna stepped to the front of the line. "Two hot chocolates, please," he said. He pulled out his wallet.

"Mint? Or regular? Marshmallows or not?" the server asked.

"Mint and marshmallows," he replied and looked at Brenna, who frowned. Probably over his comment about ambition and families and working too hard. He didn't care if he *had* put that frown on her face, she needed to hear what he thought.

"Neither," she responded to the server. "I like mine plain and I don't need the extra sugar in the marshmallows." She looked slightly uncomfortable, so he decided to explain more about his newfound attitude about work.

He'd tell her about Paul Forster. Except she saw him as a dance instructor, not a venture capitalist. Now he was the one wearing a frown.

He paid for their drinks, and they stepped away to circle the square amid the throngs of arriving people. He took a sip and burned the tip of this tongue. "Hot! Be careful."

"I'll let it cool," she promised.

"I worked with a man awhile back who dedicated his every waking moment to his new business. Paul felt driven to succeed, to make his product a household staple. He had a son and two daughters and a wife who loved and supported him."

"Jett?" came a woman's effusive call. He looked up and saw Marva give him a wave that belonged in a football stadium.

"You're gonna love meeting this woman," he said out of the corner of his mouth. Brenna grinned. "Marva, nice to see you here," he called back and waved her over.

"Marva's a favorite student of mine," he said when she arrived, breathless and happy and rosy-cheeked. "And this is Brenna," he announced. The women exchanged smiles and greetings, while he took stock of the proceedings around him. They had almost circled around to the carousel again. "Marva, I'll get you a hot chocolate, if you'd like."

"Thanks, I'd love some."

"Stay right here. I need to make a call. I'll do it while I'm in line." He pulled out his cell phone as he strode to the vendor. Jett had called his assistant, Sophia, and explained what he wanted several hours ago. But this time Jett wanted information of a more personal nature on the man behind the process. Sophia answered on the first ring.

Ignoring a greeting she said, "I can't find a thing on a Billie Adamson from Dickens or the surrounding county. There are no William Adamsons in that area."

"The breadcrumbs the guy left in the chat room lead to Dickens." Jett wasn't often wrong. He shrugged it off. "I'll check further from my end."

"Unless he doesn't own or rent a property. He could be a roommate not on the lease," she suggested. "That would make it harder to find him."

"Yes. Maybe he moved in with a woman who already had a place."

"I'll dig deeper."

"No, not tonight. You should be leaving for home by now." He had boots on the ground here and he'd keep looking. Now that he had contacts in Dickens, like Laurel and Mrs. Moore, he might have better luck.

"I'm heading out to buy presents. Do you have your list of gifts yet? Don't make me scramble last minute. I'll order more online this year. We need to have enough time for delivery."

"I'll send the list to you soon." He flashed on how much fun he'd had picking out the earmuffs for Brenna. He'd been delighted with them, and he'd bought a pair for himself on a whim. Funny, he didn't usually do whims. He didn't indulge silly impulses. Time off to chat up a woman, hanging out doing nothing constructive, laughing for no reason other than enjoying the company he was with; all those things were alien to him.

He ended his call and while he stood in line, swept the square with his gaze. He drank it all in. Quaint towns weren't his thing, but then, he'd never spent time in them. He loved what he saw here in Dickens: a gazebo for music and important speeches, a carousel, a statue, a walkway that wove in and out of the structures. In the middle stood a towering, perfectly conical pine draped in strands of unlit light bulbs.

The shops and elegant old homes that circled the square had also kept their lights off as darkness had fallen.

"One hot chocolate, please." He considered Marva's sense of style and went with what he figured she'd want. "With marshmallows." He paid for the drink and hurried back to the waiting women.

As he got closer, he saw that the crowd had come to order, and silence had built as parents shushed children all around him. Brenna waved to him to hurry. He dodged people faster.

"What's happening?" he whispered to Brenna as he passed Marva her paper cup.

Marva mouthed her thank you and turned to face the gazebo.

"We get a speech every year but this year instead of the mayor, a kid gets to throw the switch."

The speech was peppered with thank yous and the usual gratitude to the sponsors without whom the event couldn't happen. People responded with applause as their friends and family got mentions from the mayor.

"Without further ado, I invite—drum roll—Wilhelmina Adamson to power up." The crowd cheered as the teenage girl in a wheelchair flipped a switch on an electrical board.

The entire square lit up at once, and a moment later the surrounding homes and business turned on their lights, too. The tree glowed with thousands of twinkling lights. Magnificent in its glory.

Without warning, Brenna tugged his face down to hers and slammed her lips to his. He responded and gave her a one-armed hug because they were still holding their cups. When he raised his head, he smiled into the kiss thief's eyes. Then he glanced around to see most people bussing their partners on the lips.

"It's tradition," Brenna explained, "to kiss the one you're with."

"Like New Year's Eve," Marva exclaimed. "I love it!"

With that, Jett gave the older woman a smacking kiss on the cheek. She touched her face where he'd smooched it and cackled like a crow. "Thanks, Jett. It's been a while." He may have seen a tear glisten, but she blinked.

Adamson. Maybe a relative of Billie's. He'd almost missed the name, but the mayor had raised his voice to announce it.

Marva turned to say hello to people on her other side and began chatting animatedly about how nice the ceremony had been.

After a brief hello to the other people, Jett had Brenna to himself again. "You said we were about to be invaded by your aunt and grandmother. Where did they disappear to?"

Brenna shrugged. "Not sure, but you can bet I'll be grilled like a steak when I get home. They'll want every juicy bit of this evening."

"I don't want it to end, but the crowd is leaving." And he wanted more kisses, plain and simple. "Would you go to dinner with me? It's still early."

"The crowd's heading to the restaurants on the square. They'll be completely full," she said consideringly. "How about Antonelli's? It's about fifteen minutes from here and serves Italian cuisine."

"I love the way you say yes. Not only am I spending more time with you; you've already found the way to my heart. Italian is my favorite food. Bring it on!"

In the lights from the tree they stood beside, he saw her flush the prettiest pink hue he'd ever seen.

"Jett and Brenna," Marva's voice broke into their shared moment. "Harry here invited me to see the snowman building contest. Care to come along?" She raised her brows expectantly.

Harry, a man somewhere in his late sixties to early seventies stood behind her looking hopeful.

"We were discussing dinner plans," Jett said.

Harry spoke up. "I'd also like to ask Marva to join me for a bite after I see my grandchildren build their snowman." He hooked his thumb over his shoulder to indicate a direction. Jett followed with his gaze and saw a park past the square. Families were heading in that direction.

Marva tilted her head in a clear signal for Jett and Brenna to clear off. With a jaunty wave, Jett grabbed Brenna's hand and left Marva to her new friend. She'd been right about single men being in the square tonight. Maybe Marva had a sixth sense about romance, because she'd found Harry in record time.

Chapter Seven

Kissing Jett had been the smartest thing Brenna had done all day. And how sweet had it been that he'd given Marva a nice big smacker on the cheek? Brenna had seen a glow come over the woman's face when Jett had included her in the tradition. With her heart warming toward the man at her side, she walked with him to his car.

"I hope I remember the way to Antonelli's." She'd been there before, but it had been a while.

"I hope we beat the rush," he replied with a grin. "But then waiting in a line up would give me more time with you."

"Sweet talker," she teased.

He chuckled and picked up her gloved hand. He brushed his lips across it, and she wanted, desperately, to take her glove off for him. Maybe more than her glove. *Stop, you're going way too fast.* But she wasn't sure her rational self would listen. Around Jett Smith, she felt warm and different and excited, and she loved the feelings he brought out in her. Being with him made her light-hearted and she loved it.

As they reached his car, they were waylaid by Gramma and Aunt Lolly. They popped like genies out from behind a bush right beside Jett's car.

"Have you been lying in wait?" she demanded.

"Mrs. Moore and my favorite server, Laurel," Jett cut in smoothly. "Who'd have thought we'd be connected by Brenna here." Jett was suave. The confident kind of man women fawned over. These two were no exception.

Both women smiled widely. "Yes, who'd have thought?" Gramma said a little breathlessly.

Brenna gave her beloved family members the stink eye, but they didn't notice, given that they were both staring up at Jett.

"We're heading to Antonelli's for a meal. Care to join us?" He invited.

"No, no, no, we couldn't," Gramma said with a nudge to her daughter.

"We wanted to see how the square looked from a distance," Lolly said in a bald-faced lie. It was clear they wanted to ask where Brenna was headed with Jett.

"Don't wait up," Brenna repeated what she'd said at the house as she'd left. She moved around to the passenger door. Jett tapped his key fob and then opened the unlocked door for her.

"Ladies," he bid them goodnight with a silky smile and rounded the front of the car to climb inside. "I have a feeling they kept an eye on us the whole time."

"Ya think? How embarrassing," she groused. "This will only get worse when my mom, sister, and cousin arrive." Except that Trix's news would soon overshadow a minor fling of Brenna's. After all, Trix's whole life had changed while Brenna would return to her old, established life and Jett would fade into history.

Her life, such as it was, would not include the mysterious Jett Smith.

"Let's make the most of our time here, Jett." She turned in her seat to watch his face in the glow from the dashboard. His jaw held a hint of stubble and his profile looked sharp in the rosy dashboard glow.

"Absolutely," he said with a strong whiff of relief in the word. "I'm in, Brenna, for as long as you want."

His words sent a delicious shiver down her spine. Christmas in Dickens just got a whole lot more interesting.

FOR JETT, THE FOLLOWING days were a kind of magic he'd never experienced before. After working all morning, his stops at Dorrit's for an afternoon coffee became about conversation, jokes, and sitting beside Brenna on a stool while she chatted with her aunt. Laurel introduced him to all the regulars and, strangely, he began to feel as if he belonged.

After their visit in the diner, they'd head to the studio where they'd hold each other and dance the tango, rumba, salsa and more. By the time Marva arrived for her hourlong lesson, Jett and Brenna had teased and flirted and kissed each other senseless.

Their kisses were more enticing because they couldn't take their feelings any further, not with Marva arriving any minute. He wasn't sure why he didn't press for more than kisses and brief explorations with Brenna, but he wanted to take his time and get to know her first.

Brenna had quickly become the most important woman he'd ever had in his life. He didn't want anything to ruin his chance to make something bigger come out of this Christmas in Dickens.

Evenings were spent having dinner with Brenna, either out at a cozy restaurant, or at home with her grandmother. He came to learn that Mrs. Moore was a social butterfly who flitted happily from hosting book club meetings to joining friends for dinner or movies.

Brenna proved to be an avid reader of true crime. The gorier the better, she said once, and he shuddered. At least in political thrillers, assassins worked from a distance or made quick kills.

Marva reminded him of Delia, his early mentor and dear friend. In a way, spending time with Marva and including her had become his way of paying forward Delia's kindness.

The mystery of Billie Adamson had yet to be solved and he'd still not found any Adamsons living in Dickens or in the surrounding area. He'd put off asking Mrs. Moore or Laurel about the mystery man.

He should ask them about the girl who flipped the switch at the lighting ceremony. Maybe she had an older brother.

He still felt cautious about exposing his real reason for being here, but it was time he put more effort into finding Billie Adamson. After all, he'd come to Dickens for a reason and for the last few days he'd set that reason aside to spend time with Brenna.

He needed to remember his other life and his business. Sophia had made noises about him giving up this quest. That would be a first and the idea of giving up on a promising project was hard to take.

He carried a hot, heavy dish of lasagna out to the dining table for Mrs. Moore and set it down on a trivet. She appeared at his side with a knife and lifter. "Will you do the honors, Jett?"

"My pleasure." He'd picked up a crusty loaf from the bakery which Mrs. Moore sliced into. Brenna produced a bottle of nice red wine. She poured a glass for each of them while Jett sliced into the mouthwatering lasagna. "This meal smells incredible. While we eat, I have something or someone, to ask you about."

"Sounds mysterious," the older woman said with a smile. "But ask away."

They settled to their meal and after a moment, Jett decided not to share his real name or purpose here. Not yet. There'd be plenty of time to tell all after he and Brenna came to an understanding. He'd already decided he'd relocate to Manhattan when she returned to New York. That conversation needed to be private, and he didn't want to tip his hand until they were alone, and he was certain of Brenna's feelings.

"What did you want to ask me, Jett?" Brenna's grandmother asked.

"Nothing important," he hedged. "I hear there's a killer toboggan hill around here and there's snow coming overnight. Care to join me, Brenna?"

She grinned, mischief dancing in her eyes. "I haven't tobogganed in years. If you mean the hill at Holly Hill, near the inn, yes, it's a great toboggan run. I hope I still have the strength to drag a sled uphill."

"I'll take care of that," he promised. "Tomorrow afternoon then, instead of tango."

BRENNA ROLLED OFF THE toboggan into the snow, laughing. "I forgot how much fun this is," she said on heavy breath. She'd been holding it all the way down the slope from sheer excitement. A few yards away from the main path downhill, several kids were busy making snow angels. "Want to give that a try?" she asked Jett.

"You'll have to remind me how," he said with a grin. But the sneaky rotter had scooped snow into his mitten. He'd also rolled off on the other side of the toboggan.

"If you throw that at me, you're dead," she warned him and launched herself across his body. "Oof!" She huffed as she landed on the solid wall of his chest. But her hands were already busy picking up wads of snow. She smooshed his face with it and laughed like a loon.

As usual, his morning had been taken up with whatever the rest of his life was about. While she was curious about how he spent his time, she also respected his privacy. And knowing more about him, might make it harder to walk away when the time came.

As much as she wanted to see more of Jett when they left Dickens, her promotion would mean she'd work too many hours to sustain any kind of relationship. The idea exhausted her, so she avoided thinking about it most days. And they'd promised to take this time out in Dickens to have fun.

The snow melted quickly on his cheeks, and he relaxed back into the snow, inviting her to snuggle closer as she leaned over him. "Brenna," he whispered as he drew her head down to his. She kissed him, here, in the bright light of day, her mouth moving silkily over his, bringing heat to them both.

"I want to share more than this time with you," he murmured against her ear. "I've never felt this way before."

"That's sweet of you to say, Jett. I feel the same." But she'd witnessed many Christmas romances in Dickens before. "Something about this town brings out the best in people, but afterward, not everyone can maintain what they shared here. We need to remember that our lives will pull us back into the hustle."

His eyes shuttered and his face blanked at her reminder. "You're right. Things will change when you go back to New York."

She pushed up and off him and the sky darkened with clouds. "Looks like more snow," she said. They both brushed off their ski suits and stamped snow off their boots. The family kept old boots and coats at Gramma's for the coldest days. Dickens wasn't about the latest fashions, not when tradition ruled. "My old snow boots are worn out. My toes are freezing."

"Mine too. Your grandfather's old boots have next to no lining left in them. Let's call it a day," Jett said and grabbed the rope to pull the toboggan to his car. "If I ever come back here for Christmas, I'll bring warmer boots."

Brenna trudged silently beside him, letting the clouds overhead shadow her mood. They were halfway through their time in Dickens and soon her mom, sister, and cousin would arrive. "Once the rest of the family shows up, we won't have as much time to ourselves," she said in a melancholy tone.

"You sound as bummed about that as I am." He raised his mittens in surrender. "Not that I'm not looking forward to meeting your family, but I've cherished this time alone with you."

"Me, too. I've relaxed and rested, and I haven't thought about work in at least three hours." She pretended to read a watch. It was true. And yesterday, she'd felt the same way. She took his hand, mitten to mitten, wishing it were warm enough for skin on skin.

"Kiss me again. I like this relaxed you. Rested suits you."

"Smooth talker," she teased but kissed him as requested. When she pulled away, her heart rate had sped up and her cheeks were warm. "Jett," she whispered. "I really like you."

"Feeling's mutual, Brenna."

Chapter Eight

December twentieth dawned like any other day in Dickens. Jett went about his morning as usual, still no closer to finding Billie Adamson. Odd, but his failure to find the man didn't eat at him as he would have expected. Maybe because he'd already sent Sophia home for the holidays. Maybe having Brenna in his life had mellowed his ambition. All felt right in his world as the clock moved inexorably toward the arrival of the James clan.

And then later that morning when they arrived, it felt like a bomb went off. He'd never seen an explosion of people and cheery greetings before. Not like this.

Jett was quickly overcome with the blast of happy these people brought to Mrs. Moore's front door. Brenna had insisted he be with her to welcome her parents and sister—Kylie or Kayley—followed closely by her cousin, Trix, and Aunt Laurel.

Introductions were a nightmare. Usually when in a crowd, he had Sophia with him, taking notes and running interference. She blocked a lot of pushy entrepreneurs desperate to get his attention. He was often alone in a crowd and wasn't expected to perform or conform to a pre-conceived notion.

Carloads of Christmas gifts were being unloaded from two cars and carried into the house. Names were repeated and relationships explained. He hoped no one quizzed him afterward.

"Merry Christmas! This is Jett, Brenna's new boyfriend. Isn't he handsome?" Gramma announced.

When they heard this declaration, Brenna's parents stopped dead in their tracks in the front hall, blocking the stream of traffic. Her mother,

Jennifer, was an older version of Brenna, while her dad, Reggie, had passed her his hair and eye color.

Her family looked him up, down, and across. The women seemed pleased with what they saw, but Brenna's father was another story.

Brenna stood immediately behind her parents with a pile of gifts, wrapped and bagged in bright Christmas red, green, silver and gold. She grimaced comically and rolled her eyes as she mouthed *sorry*.

Reggie James frowned and grunted until his wife gave him an elbow in the side. He moved past Jett with bags of groceries.

"Mom, shuffle along please," Brenna pleaded. "You can inspect Jett after we get all this stuff inside." Her eyes begged his forgiveness.

"I'll squeeze by," Jett offered, "and get the luggage." He leaned on the wall as Jennifer and Brenna walked through to the living room. Brenna's bright, happy smile was reward enough for his agreeing to be here. He hadn't wanted to interfere with the reunion, but Gramma, Laurel, and Brenna had pressed, saying he was one of them now and they'd hate to think of him in his place alone when they had lots of room and extra food.

As Jett walked to the back of the first car to get to the trunk, he saw Trix, Laurel, and a woman who must be Kayley conferring quietly and tensely behind Laurel's SUV. Whatever they talked about was family business and he moved quickly to lift the two wheeled suitcases out of the open trunk. He acknowledged Laurel's tremulous smile with a brief nod and hotfooted it back to the relative quiet of the parental inspection awaiting him.

Reggie waited on the front porch eyeing him as if Jett were a midnight intruder. Much easier to deal with than three women with their heads together looking tense and upset.

Clearly, there were things about being in a family he'd never understand, but he figured his appearance here could prove the least interesting part of the visit. Maybe Brenna had wanted him along for a buffer. He drew the suitcases around to his front and waited while Reggie looked him over skeptically. Jett considered moving up the stairs to make the older man move aside, but chose to remain on the ground, looking up.

Reggie's gaze raked him. Jett stood a bit taller, giving the older man a respectful look. "Boyfriend, eh?" Reggie grumped.

"Seems so."

"Been together long?"

"A couple of weeks."

"What do you do for a living?"

"Right now, I'm teaching dance." This was tricky. Lying to Brenna's father felt wrong, but Jett wasn't completely ready to give up his search for Billie Adamson despite his cooled ambition. He planned to pick up the search again after the new year. Until Jett found the man, he needed to keep his real identity a secret.

"Leave the man alone," Jennifer said and tapped her husband on the shoulder. "You've got your answers."

Reggie nodded and stepped aside to give Jett room to pass by with the suitcases. Instead of helping with the luggage, the older man wandered down to the sidewalk to where Jett had parked. Reggie walked around the car Jett had rented. "Looks too nice for a dance instructor," came the gruff comment.

Jett ignored the observation and carried the luggage to the second floor where he set it down. From up here, he looked below to see the family milling about. The chatter of greetings and compliments on the decorations rose merrily to where he stood. Like the rare times he'd been in a foster home, Christmas meant staying apart from the rest of the family members. He'd rarely felt included.

"Jett come on down here," Kayley called putting a lie to his memory. "It's our tradition to get the tree as soon as we arrive so we can decorate it tomorrow. We all go, and you're coming too. Besides, you can do the heavy lifting," she said with a sly wink.

"I'll carry the tree," Reggie said in a growl, "like always."

"With Jett to help, we can get a bigger one," Brenna's mother chimed in.

All but Jett seemed to be in on the joke and howled with laughter at Reggie's expense. Jett had never been to a Christmas tree farm. He didn't know what to look for in a tree. Like most things to do with this holiday, he'd go along with whatever Brenna wanted.

"GRIDLEY MEADOWS FARM hasn't changed," Brenna commented. There were still rows and rows of trees of various sizes. The family had fanned out to optimize their choices. Brenna suspected everyone wanted to give her and Jett a few minutes alone. She reached for Jett's hand, and he stopped and turned to her, his eyes alight with joy. It was almost as if this was a new experience for him. Laughter rose from all around them, interspersed with cheers and calls about finding the perfect tree.

"Mom's right," she said to Jett. "With you here maybe we'll get a bigger tree. Dad won't like needing help but he's not getting any younger."

"Happy to help anyway I can. I'm not sure your dad likes me, though."

She mugged a face at her father's foolishness. It wasn't as if Jett was serious about her. "You're being a good sport. I appreciate it. My dad is cautious with any men who show up in my and Kayley's lives. I'm sorry if he's made you uncomfortable." But her mother had seemed to take to Jett and had accepted her private apology for skipping Thanksgiving. Brenna had squirmed when she'd explained about work and her promotion, but her mom had waved her off. Which made Brenna feel even more guilty.

"I get it," Jett said. "You dad wasn't impressed with my teaching the tango." He tipped his forehead to hers.

She leaned back and made a line of her lips and searched his gaze. "I'm not sure he believed you after seeing your expensive coat and car."

Not to mention his designer boots which he'd left behind in favor of borrowing her grandfather's old ones again. "Is there something you're not telling me about your career?"

He drew in a deep breath. "You're right, I'm not telling you everything. I'm not usually a dance instructor, but I enjoy it and I decided it would make a good cover for my real purpose for visiting Dickens."

"Real purpose?" Her mind skipped from private investigator, to mercenary, to witness protection, to secret agent. None of which suited the man she'd come to care about. "Explain, because this is confusing."

He nodded. "I'm what some might call an angel investor and I'm here to find a young man I believe has a marvelous new process. I believe he needs my help to get it into production and eventually to market."

"This Billie Adamson you've asked about?"

"You're observant and smart and I apologize for not clueing you in before this."

"Are you like those people on TV who help entrepreneurs on that reality show?"

"Not exactly. They're running their own business empires and don't mind the limelight. I prefer to stay anonymous until I'm sure an invention is viable. I do my own searches and keep a low profile."

"You must work hard. I recall you mentioning ambition destroying families. Is that why you're single?"

"I wouldn't put it that way. When we talked about your long hours at work, I thought of my last protégé and how he lost his family. Paul wanted his wife and children to have whatever they wanted. In the end, what they wanted was him and he didn't see the wedge he'd let grow between them."

"What happened to them?"

"I advised him to sell the company and sort things out. He took a long time to decide what was most important because he'd taken his wife and children for granted." Jett shrugged. "In the end, he chose love over business. But he took weeks longer than he should have. I wasn't sure he'd ever figure it out. I got word this morning from my assistant, Sophia. The family is spending Christmas together and he's decided to sell his business." His lips tilted up at the corners and his eyes brimmed with pride.

Suddenly her phone blew up with texts and pictures as the rest of the family found trees they liked. "Looks like the competition's begun."

"We haven't found a tree yet." He looked panicked, his eyes darting from tree to tree. "There's one! It's perfect. Like the kind you see in the movies. Can we get that one?" He voice sounded like an excited four-year-old's.

She turned and tracked his gaze. "Easy there, big fella. We usually decide as a family but that's a beauty." She snapped a picture and sent it to the group. "Now we wait."

"While we wait, there's something I want to do."

"What's that?"

"Kiss you. I haven't had a chance all morning."

She pulled her hand out of her mitten to press a finger to his lips. "First, tell me if Jett Smith is your real name." As soon as he said he wanted anonymity she'd wondered if he'd hidden things from her.

"Somers. I'm Jett Somers. And I want to tell you all about me. For you, Brenna James, I'm an open book."

Her phone pinged wildly with congratulatory messages. "We won. We're taking the tree you want."

He pulled her in tight and close and kissed her. Their lips warmed against the cold, but she shivered as desire rose. Warmed from the inside she whispered, "Jett, hold me." She wanted to say much more, to talk about a future, but fear stopped her.

He was wooing her. He wanted her in his life. But what if she failed him? What if she went back to work and lost him in the crushing load of responsibility?

A throat cleared and he raised his head and smiled. "We've been caught," he murmured for her ears only.

"We don't mean to interrupt, but you're blocking our way and we want to chop that tree before some other family gets it." It was her sister's voice, full of amusement.

Brenna shifted her gaze from Jett's to Kayley's. Her father stood immediately behind her, holding an axe.

"My father has an axe in his hands."

Jett stepped back and put his hands high in the air. "We're done here," he declared loudly.

"Good," her father said. "Now, out of my way, I've got chopping to do." He brushed past Kayley and advanced on them. "You," he said to Jett, "watch your feet. I wouldn't want to miss the base of the tree." He gave Jett an amused glance on his way by.

"That smile he gave me looked scary," he said. "I'm hanging back here until the chopping's done."

Chapter Nine

With the best-looking tree on the lot tied to the roof of Laurel's SUV, Jett marveled at how much fun he'd had. He held Brenna's hand as they trooped across the parking lot toward the old red barn dedicated to food and drink. Once inside, he saw more Christmas decorations like wreaths and lawn ornaments for sale.

Joy eased through Jett at how simple Christmas could be with a family who cared about each other. Until now, the season had been a backdrop for his time with Brenna. He'd noticed the lights and seasonal decorations, but they hadn't warmed him until now. "This is one of the best days I've ever had," he said into her ear.

The bright smile she gave him went through to his soul.

After ordering their hot drinks and plates of cookies they gathered at the round tables by the woodstove. The cookies were shaped like Christmas trees, stars, and sleds. He had his share and then some. Buttery goodness filled his mouth and contentment filled his heart. Even Reggie had thawed a little.

"I'm glad you're having fun," Brenna responded warmly. "I am, too. I didn't want to give up our alone time, but we'll manage. Now that they've met you, I feel lighter and freer. I hate to say it this way because it's corny, but Christmas is special in Dickens, and we all relax and enjoy the season here." Bry had been right to push her to come home for Christmas. He'd be pleased to hear how well his ploy had worked.

"I want to talk to you. We need some of that alone time." He'd missed her, even though they spent lots of time together. Her family was great, but they were always *there*.

A woman's chiding voice broke over their heads interrupting his thoughts. "Wilhelmina Adamson, get down from there."

They all looked over to see the young teen who'd thrown the switch at the lighting ceremony. She stood up from her wheelchair to reach a Christmas bulb from a high shelf. She wobbled a bit but seemed determined to get that one special bulb.

"Billie," the woman cried again. "I'll get it. Sit down."

The line of people waiting for service parted to let the woman through. Just in time she clasped the wobbling girl around the waist and helped her back into her chair. "But, Mom, I can get it and I don't want you to see what I'm buying for you."

Billie. This was Billie Adamson. Not a young man, but a teenage girl. She'd disappeared from the chat room completely and without warning. Jett had spent weeks looking for the wrong person.

He stood without a word. He had to get to her.

Her mother fussed and clucked over her while Billie looked stubborn and disappointed. "Mom, stop," she said firmly. An obstinate purse of her lips overtook her pretty face. Her short braid rested at her frayed coat collar.

He had to approach them. It was clear this *contretemps* between mother and daughter had ruined a happy outing and that meant he'd run out of time. He walked over, leaving Brenna in mid-conversation.

"Mrs. Adamson?" he asked quietly. The woman, frazzled, looked up at him quickly and then went back to settling her daughter.

"It's Miss Barnes. What do you want?"

"It's about Billie, here. I met her online and—"

"You're the guy?" She interrupted with the force of a raging rhino. "A grown man? Here to do what with my little girl?"

"What? Wait!" A murmur grew around them as sick horror settled in Jett's gut. "No!" he said just as forcefully. "This isn't what you think. I didn't know she was a girl, or young. I believed it was an adult, a scientist, in that chat room."

"Trying to get her to tell you where she lived, asking about her schooling? How stupid do you think we are? I got her offline as fast as I could."

He raised his palms to his face and dragged them down in frustration and horror. She believed he was the worst kind of man. "No. All of this is wrong. Billie, did I ever talk about anything that made you uncomfortable?"

She stared at her lap and shook her head. "No," she whispered. Louder, she said, "Mom, let's go, you're embarrassing me."

He took in the condition of the wheelchair. It was old, the seat back worn. Miss Barnes' clothes were past their prime. This woman was struggling financially and needed to hear what he had to say. He pressed his card into Billie's hand. "I want to understand your process with the batteries. That's all. I can help."

Miss Barnes took the card from Billie's hand and glared at him. "She's always got her head in science journals and the like. I can't make sense of any of it."

"MOM! I want to leave." She cast Jett a look of utter humiliation.

He nodded and cleared a path for them. "Please call and we can talk about Billie's future and yours. Do a search online about me. Dig deep. You'll understand who I am and why I'm here. I promise this will change things for you." And the world, he hoped.

When he looked toward the tables for Brenna and her family, they were gone.

"BRENNA, HE'S A DANCE instructor. Why waste your time?" her father blustered, still incensed by what he'd overheard. He'd turned an alarming shade of burgundy and that was the only reason Brenna had hurried out of the gift shop.

No way on Earth Jett was an internet stalker of young teens. Of course not. But trying to get through to her father when he ranted this way was a fool's game. Her mother shook her head when Brenna opened her mouth to speak.

Fine, she'd say nothing about the false accusation until her father had calmed down. She wouldn't get through to him, no matter what she said.

"Jett and I are a holiday flirtation, nothing more." The words felt like acid on her tongue and belied all that had passed between them. She worried Jett might think she believed that girl's mother. A quick end to their Christmas romance was for the best, but she had to tell him she believed he was a good man. She refused to part ways on such a sour note.

Her eyes smarted with tears as they climbed into their vehicles and left. She took one glance out the back window and saw Jett, standing alone in the cold, watching them drive away. She waved at him, once.

He didn't wave back.

Her mother turned to look at her with narrowed eyes and gave her one sharp shake of her head. Trix and Kayley flashed looks between each other. Brenna felt certain they had a few things to say about Jett, too.

An hour later, with no word from Jett, Brenna settled at the dining room table. Gramma's wonderful homemade chicken noodle soup fragranced the air, but she couldn't bear to try it. It would feel too normal, and nothing about this past hour felt normal, and she couldn't bear to eat. Her spoon rested in her hand, unused.

Trix smiled at her in a "got your back, cousin," kind of way and cleared her throat. "I have something to tell you all," she began.

Everyone raised their faces toward Trix, and Brenna set her spoon down beside her cooling bowl of soup.

"I'm getting divorced."

The bald statement completely shifted the focus from Jett to Trix, and Brenna went to her cousin and gave her the biggest hug ever.

Brenna had heard the news from Aunt Lolly and had had a couple of weeks to see that this situation had a silver lining. "From now on Trix you'll be free to pursue your dreams. Please get back to your art," she said softly. "No more hiding your light under a bushel. No more being at Dale's beck and call."

Trix nodded shakily. "You're right," she said with a tremulous smile. "I've been thinking along those lines myself," Trix responded for everyone at the table. "Don't be sad." She held up her hands. "And please let's not talk about what a bad guy Dale is for doing what he's done. Good riddance."

Aunt Lolly whispered the truth in Gramma's ear. Trix's husband was having a child with another woman. Brenna saw the exact moment the idea exploded behind Gramma's eyes. She coughed as if the truth was too hard to swallow.

"Oh, dear Trix," she said, reaching across the table. "Good riddance is right. My brave girl."

With that, her parents looked from face to face for clarification, but Trix said it out loud before anyone else could. "He found a younger woman to start a family with. Good luck to her."

Trix had deliberately stepped up to take the heat of the family's attention and concern away from her and Jett. Brenna would be grateful for the rest of her life.

JETT WAITED IN HIS car an hour after the disaster at Gridley Meadows Farm. His nerves were taut with dread, as the seconds ticked by. He'd wanted more than anything to chase after Brenna and her family to explain away what they'd overheard but he couldn't. That conversation would take far too long and deservedly so. When he spoke to Brenna, he needed to give her his full attention. The world needed the magic that Billie had stumbled on, and Jett couldn't leave the matter unresolved. But the longer he went without contacting Brenna, the worse he felt. He sent her a quick text apologizing for the confusion and to please call when she could.

He nervously tapped his index fingers on the steering wheel as he waited for a call from Brenna or from Billie's mother, Miss Barnes. Both women needed heavy explanations, and both deserved his undivided attention.

His ringtone blasted through the chilly air. He checked the screen. Not Brenna. He answered immediately. "Jett Somers.

"This is Juliet Barnes."

"Miss Barnes, thank you for calling me. You have no idea how important it is."

"We did the internet search on you at the neighbor's place." She sniffed. "Billie made me."

"We need to talk. The three of us. Name a place."

Ms. Barnes gave him an address and two hours to stew over what he'd say. He'd text Brenna again and meet with her now, somewhere away from her family.

Before he hit send, his phone rang again. "Brenna," he answered. "Thank God. We need to talk. I can explain. I'm a wreck." He loved her so much and now he could lose her.

"Calm down," she said softly. "Right back at you, Jett. I'm a wreck, too. Tell me where you are, and I'll come there."

"I'm parked in the square, in front of Dickens Hardware." The word hurry dangled on his tongue, but he bit it back.

"I'll be there in five minutes. Hold on and wait for me."

He set his forehead on his steering wheel while a hundred voices screamed at him. "You're a loser." "No one will ever love you." "Don't come crying to me." Were among some of his favorites when he felt overwhelmed. He pulled them out whenever he wasn't sure he could achieve what he needed to do.

But then, softly, a whisper came to his rescue. "You can do this, Jett. Try once more. Just a little straighter. Keep working, it'll come." Delia's whisper grew stronger, louder until it drowned out the nasty shouts and jabs from other kids in the system and the group homes. Those other voices had come close to breaking him before he aged out. But Delia had put a stop to all that. She'd guided him through his rockiest years and when life and his classes in college had threatened to beat him down, she'd been there.

Even after she'd passed, she'd been there. Her voice came to him at times like this. She'd left him a home and enough money to get a start in life, and he'd be grateful until his dying breath.

Chapter Ten

Brenna found Jett hunched over his steering wheel and when she tapped on his window, he startled as if he'd been sleeping. When he saw her, he grimaced. She hurried around to the passenger side and climbed in beside him.

Jett said nothing but drew her into his arms and rested his head on her shoulder like a child. "I'm not like that, Brenna. I'm not a guy who tries to lure young girls on the internet."

"I know," she said quietly and firmly to get through his anguish. "I never believed it for a moment." She lifted his head to face her. "You mentioned Billie to me before. A man who had a secret, ugly, agenda would never say her name or tell anyone they were looking for her."

He blinked and tilted his head as if awed. "I swear I thought when we were online that Billie was a young man," he said fervently. "I assumed he was a science major in university. That was the school I asked him—her—about." He shook his head. "I can't believe this happened—I mean—I knew the person was young just by the language, but a young teen? She's what, twelve or thirteen? No. I didn't have a clue. Her command of science jargon alone, made me assume an adult was talking."

She nodded to encourage him. "Go on," she coaxed. "I need to hear all of it."

"The young man I chatted with went silent right after I asked about school. Now I see why. Billie's mother—whose name is Barnes, not Adamson—must have read our chats and put a stop to them. Rightly so. I'd do the same if it were a child of mine."

"Yes. Me, too."

"But this discovery of Billie's is important, Brenna. It could change the future of the planet."

"That big?"

"Yes. That big."

"Then, what's next? My grandmother recognized Miss Barnes from around town. She said the girl's father comes from an old, established family from Philadelphia. Very wealthy. He's refused to acknowledge Billie. His lawyers keep delaying a paternity test, but you only have to see him to know he's her father. Miss Barnes has struggled with Billie's medical expenses for years. She's had many legal battles and she still gets no help." Brenna watched understanding and disgust enter Jett's gaze as she explained the girl's circumstances.

"They need me as much as the world needs Billie's process." He set his jaw. "You've explained why I couldn't find any local Adamsons. Since Miss Barnes gave her daughter her father's name, it was impossible to make the connection."

"I have their address if you want to go." She gave him the address and he smiled.

"We've spoken," he said, sounding pleased. "I've got another hour to wait for my appointment. She's invited me to her home. I assumed the address she gave me was somewhere public, but she's checked me out and understands I'm not a threat to her daughter." His eyes brimmed with relief.

She felt the same relief. "We'll go see them together. I'll explain who I am. Maybe Juliet Barnes will feel better if I'm there."

"I can't express my gratitude. Brenna—"

"Sh." She stopped him with a kiss. "This isn't the time for our conversation. Let's focus on Billie and Juliet for now."

"You're right." He blew out a breath and grinned. "What do you want to do for the next hour?"

They strolled arm in arm around the square. The Trim-a-Tree store was filled with shoppers, but Jett wanted to go inside.

"I need to buy something," he said with an air of secrecy. Once inside, he studied the ornaments for sale on the trees. Finally, he picked one off and smiled. "I've found the perfect one," he announced. He palmed it so she couldn't see it.

"What have you got there?"

"Na-unh, not telling. But I will say that this is the first tree ornament I've ever purchased."

"Really?"

He nodded and his gaze went inward. "Christmas is kind of foreign to me. At least, the spirit is." He dipped his head and ran his hand over his hair to the back of his neck. Jett looked uncomfortably adorable, like a child with a guilty confession to make. "This is the first time I've ever felt the spirit. When I was a kid, my life was different from yours and the season was either a long bender for my foster parents or I was in a group home and the cheer seemed phony and forced."

She grieved for the loss of his childhood. "Jett," she said softly and tugged on his upper arm. She pressed her forehead to his.

He shrugged. "You have no idea what you've given me, Brenna."

"Jett," she crooned again, her heart twisting. She kissed his forehead, the tip of his nose and then, his mouth. To comfort? To help him heal? To show how she felt? Maybe all three. "You've shared yourself with me, finally. And it is the most wonderful gift of all."

She wanted to say she loved him, but they didn't have time. He needed to sort out his situation with Billie and her mother. "We should go."

He nodded and headed to the cash desk to pay for his ornament.

BILLIE AND HER MOTHER, Juliet Barnes, appeared to live in a house converted to separate units. On the side of the wide veranda steps sat a homemade ramp; built to accommodate Billie's chair, Jett supposed. "That ramp's too steep," he said. "It would be hard to push the chair up there."

Billie's mother opened the front door and bade them enter a narrow hallway. A staircase went to the second floor, but she took them into an open door on the right. She flashed a quick, curious look at Brenna. "I made hot chocolate. It's Billie's favorite."

He flashed Brenna a broad smile. "We love it, too. Thanks for seeing me, Miss Barnes. This is my..." Jett trailed away because he wasn't sure what to call his relationship with Brenna.

"Girlfriend," Brenna supplied matter-of-factly as she unwound her scarf. Her voice was breezy, and the ease of her tone made him sigh with relief inside.

"I figured. You look like a couple." She led the way into a front room where Billie waited. "You can call me Juliet. And you already know I call Wilhelmina, Billie."

"Mom, I hate my real name," Billie said with a shy smile. "Hi, Mr. Somers. I'm sorry about earlier. My mom says it's dumb to be on the internet so much. She says it's ruining my brain." She tapped the arms of her chair. "But what else am I supposed to do?"

Juliet waved them into the sofa and as they took their seats, she spoke. "I've checked you out, Mr. Somers and I was wrong about you. You really are here to talk to us about Billie's science stuff. We saw what you've done for other inventors and small businesses." She flashed her daughter a nervous smile. "That's right, isn't it, Billie? You invented something."

"Miss Barnes," Jett said. "I understand how you could see things the way you did. And if I were a father, I'd do whatever I needed to do to protect my child." Her grateful smile meant the world.

Billie broke in with a reply to her mother's question. "I may have stumbled on a process to double the life of batteries, Mom. It's a special coating that goes under the outer shell." She shrugged. "Want to see?" she directed the question to everyone and then headed out of the room.

Jett jumped up first. He followed her past what appeared to be her mother's room, through the kitchen and to a back room. Half-bedroom-half-laboratory the room had once been a sun porch. "You must find it cold in here."

"In the winter I sleep with my mom, but yeah, it's cold."

First thing he'd do was get them out of this place. "How did you get your hands on all these batteries?" The litter on the tabletop gave him pause. She'd been dismantling batteries of all kinds. This couldn't be healthy. She needed a proper lab with proper gear.

"I harvest them from worn out stuff people give me."

He felt the presence of the two women behind him. "You recycle," he said, coaxing Billie to continue.

"Yes."

"You realize what this means?" His heart beat a wild tattoo. They were on the cusp of greatness. Climate saving greatness.

"Yes," Billie said solemnly, "I understand what it will mean if it works like I think it will."

"And now?"

"My mom canceled our Wi-Fi." The look of frustration on her face made him hold back a grin. Beneath this confident, brilliant girl, lay the heart of a teenager in full rebellion. "I prayed you'd find a way to come here, to figure out where I lived. I had to be careful about what I said, because she'd check sooner or later. She always does. But she was working nights right then. I had a bit of time to give you clues. I never thought she'd take away our Wi-Fi. My mom can be tough." She leaned closer. "And she holds grudges."

He chuckled. "In the giftshop, your mom made it clear what she'd decided about me. She was so loud my girlfriend's family left." He considered what Billie said. "But how did you know I wasn't a competitor or someone wanting to steal your process?"

"I didn't care. This is super important and bigger than me. Or you."

The heart of a lion. That's what Billie Adamson had. He turned toward the women standing behind him. Brenna's eyes glistened with tears and Juliet looked ashamed.

"I'm sorry," Juliet said. "I'll make things right with Brenna's family. But Billie? Why didn't you explain what you were working on? I'd have listened."

Billie shook her head. "No, you wouldn't have. You said a long time ago that girls aren't supposed to be good at science. You want to force me to do other things."

"Oh, no." Juliet rushed by Jett and kneeled by her daughter's chair. "Oh, sweetheart. I had no idea I was holding you back. That I did all that." She sobbed once then gathered Billie into a hug.

Brenna touched Jett's hand and he opened to clasp her fingers. She tugged and he followed her back to the kitchen. Mother and daughter needed a few minutes.

THREE DAYS LATER, CHRISTMAS Eve dawned brightly. There'd been a fresh fall of snow overnight and the town of Dickens seemed full of promise and delight. Jett rose quickly and ate a rushed breakfast of coffee and an energy bar. He had gifts to buy and wrap and take to Mrs. Moore's house to put under the tree.

He'd never felt like this before. He'd call it giddy but that seemed too feminine. Jazzed, maybe. Yes, jazzed felt right. He was jazzed for Christmas. Opening the window, he stuck his head outside to breathe deeply of the fresh, crisp air.

Already, he could see that shoppers were bustling around the square and urgency filled him. What if they got to all the good stuff before him? His competitiveness rose and he threw on his coat, boots, scarf, and his candy cane earmuffs.

No one would be a better Christmas gift buyer than Jett Somers. No way. No how.

At Trim-A-Tree he started off by buying a huge red velvet sack so he could carry all his purchases.

For Gramma, he bought a church for her Victorian Christmas village. Reggie would get a new scarf in Christmas red. For Jennifer he picked out a crystal Christmas angel with gold wings and halo. Laurel would have a day at the spa with her daughter, Trix. And Kayley would be treated to a weekend getaway of her choosing.

Marva. Funny, lovable Marva deserved a cruise for singles of a certain age. He felt dead certain she'd love it. But to be absolutely sure this was the right gift for his lively friend, he had a call to make.

He could hardly wait to see their expressions when they received their gifts in the morning.

With Brenna's help Juliet and Billie had found a home that was completely accessible and would move in January second. He'd personally seen to everything they'd need in the coming months. That had meant too little time spent with Brenna, but things would slow down now that he'd sorted out his commitment with Billie and Juliet.

After dinner tonight, he planned a special moment with Brenna, and he hoped for the best outcome.

Life was grand. Christmas in Dickens was more, better, than anything he could have imagined.

BRENNA CALLED BRY FIRST thing in the morning on Christmas Eve. He'd left a message the night before and had sounded buoyant and happy. She hoped that meant he had good news for her.

"Brenna, I'm glad you called back quickly. How's it going in Hicksville, USA? Full of the Christmas spirit?"

Was she? Yes. Christmas had woven a cocoon around her life, made her joyous again. And in that cocoon with her, was Jett. The last few days had been a whirlwind for them both, but Christmas Day was tomorrow, and they'd have a whole day without any commitments to anyone outside the family. The family she felt excited to share with him.

"Yes, Bry. I'm happy and stress-free for the first time in too long." She remembered she'd meant to tell him something. "And I give you all the credit. Thank you for sending me here ahead of time. It's been perfect in more ways than I can count."

"Great! That means you'll be ready to come back and take over as Marketing Director. It was close, but I convinced the board you're the one we need at the helm."

"Thank you. This promotion means a lot to me." And it did. Having this offer gave her more confidence in her abilities and she felt the last of her apprehension about her career drift away. Her future fell into place, and she couldn't wait to tell Jett. "Go have Christmas with your family, Bry. That's what I'll be doing. I'll see you in January. Merry Christmas and Happy New Year."

"Merry Christmas, Brenna." He sounded distracted, as if his mind had already moved onto the next thing on his agenda.

She wondered how often she used to feel like that, and sound like him.

Chapter Eleven

Jett picked up Marva at her hotel at three o'clock that afternoon. She'd dressed for the occasion in bright red boots, green leggings, and a gold sparkly dress. He refrained from telling her she looked like an elf and smiled all the way to the Moore house where the group waited. He'd put Marva's hostess gift and bottle of wine with his red sack in the trunk.

"This will be a fun evening," she bubbled beside him as he parked on the street. Like effervescence, she sparkled and shone her excitement. "Thank you for asking them to include me," she said suddenly sober and endearing. "It means a lot to me not to be alone tonight."

"I couldn't have Christmas without my favorite student," he said. "After dinner, I convinced Mrs. Moore to break with tradition this once."

"I'm shocked. Maybe appalled. The people of Dickens are sticklers for tradition."

He laughed. "You're right. But this might become a new tradition." He couldn't make her wait any longer and he was bursting to tell her anyway. "We're heading over to the studio to dance this evening."

"You feel like dancing?"

"Don't you?" he laughed.

"Always," she agreed with a chuckle that reminded him of Delia. He knew his old friend would approve of his incongruous friendship with Marva.

He climbed out and hustled to the passenger door to help Marva alight from the car. He heard a call from the veranda and saw the whole family waiting and waving and calling out greetings. He and Marva waved back, and then he popped open the trunk to gather his gift sack and her things.

As he walked up the shoveled path toward the welcoming group, Brenna stepped to the front and became his sole focus. Her happy smile meant the world to him, and he filled with warmth and love just looking at her.

The rest of the afternoon continued with happy games and carolers at the door. The house smelled of turkey and gravy and casseroles.

"Dinner will be earlier today than usual. Jett has a surprise for us all," Mrs. Moore announced. All eyes turned to him. "We're going dancing at the studio this evening. Doesn't that sound like fun?" she added. They all cheered.

Jett hadn't felt this accepted since Delia took him in.

There wasn't one family member who didn't like to dance. He'd found a tribe of likeminded people who welcomed him. *Delia would've loved this family.*

Brenna remained by his side throughout the afternoon and early dinner. He wanted to take her hand and lead her away to a quiet spot, but that would ruin his surprise, and he'd learned that giving was better than receiving.

Later he parked in front of the studio. The common was empty of vehicles and only one person walked their dog near the park. "Dickens looks like a picture right now," he commented in a hushed tone.

"Fresh snow on the tree boughs always makes it special," Brenna pointed out. Fat flakes wafted gently to gather on the tops of the old-fashioned lamps. The parking meters looked as if they wore white pointed hats.

Under the snow on the tree boughs, lights sent out a soft yellow glow and he knew the air would be quiet.

Marva spoke reverently from the backseat. "This is amazing."

They weren't the only car with occupants on the block.

Marva spoke again. "That looks like Harry's car. He told me he'd be spending the evening with his family."

"I called him today and he was happy to be here. For you, Marva." Jett's surprise for his friend was going off with a hitch.

"Oh, my..." her voice trailed away.

"For once, she's speechless," Jett teased. Happiness flowed through him as Harry climbed out of his car and walked over. He opened the back door for Marva.

Make that gift a cruise for two.

More cars arrived bearing the rest of Brenna's family and everyone trooped up the stairs to Tiny Tim's.

Inside the studio, Mrs. Moore started the music and Harry and Marva and Reggie and Jennifer began a tango.

Brenna flowed into Jett's arms as if she were meant just for him. He held her and crowed inside at the brush of her leg against his as they moved effortlessly across the floor. He maneuvered her into a shadowed corner by a pillar and pulled her to a stop.

"Brenna, I have to tell you how I feel about you," he started. "I know you want your promotion and how much it means to you. It's asking a lot, but please let me be part of your life for the few hours you're not at work." He'd take any amount of time just as long as she spent it with him. "I have a place in Manhattan. It used to be Delia's."

"I got the promotion, Jett. I heard today." She smiled up into his eyes.

"That's great. I'm not surprised." What would this mean for him? For them? She slid her palm to his cheek, and he froze at her touch, afraid of what might come.

"You must know my feelings for you, too. I love you, Jett Somers. And I want you in my life, too. I refused the promotion. I can't go back to that kind of stress. That isn't the life I want."

"What *do* you want, Brenna? Tell me it's what I want, too."

She tapped her chin and gave him a shy lift of her lips. "If you want marriage and children and a wife who works part-time, then we're on the same page."

"No can do. If we're negotiating, then I have another idea. Marriage, children, and you work with me on whatever marketing we need for Billie's business. That idea just came to me. I hope it works for you."

"It works for me," she said, and Jett pulled her tight against his chest for a kiss to last a lifetime.

"Hey, you two, get back to dancing. You're too close for the tango," her father called with a mock growl from across the room.

Jett and Brenna looked over to see Reggie linked arm in arm with Jennifer. They were both smiling, heads tilted together. The image of what he wanted to create for his future.

Jett gazed with all the love he had at the woman in his arms; the woman who would give him the family he never knew he craved, and said, "We begin."

The End

I HOPE YOU LOVED *The Tinsel Tango*. The town of Dickens is home to a wonderful cast of characters. Dickens was created for the Christmas season of 2020, in an anthology of short stories. Readers loved the town so much that six authors decided to write longer romances set in the same quintessential New England town.

If you choose your books based on reviews, I hope you'll pay it forward and share your thoughts on *The Tinsel Tango*. A sentence or two on how you felt when you closed the book would be fabulous.

The next books in this trilogy are **The Rumball Rumba** and **The Winterland Waltz** available through Books2Read, a handy **FREE** service that links you to your favorite store. Tell them once where you prefer to purchase (for Kindle, Apple, Kobo, Nook and more) and you will always be taken to that store, regardless of the author you purchase. So whenever you see a Books2Read link, you can trust that you'll be buying from a retailer you want to support. This link is one and done, at no cost to you!

Check out https://books2read.com/RumballRumba and https://books2read.com/WinterlandWaltz

If you prefer to browse bookstores, please request staff to order copies of the titles you'd like to read.

To learn more about upcoming releases and special deals, sign up for Bonnie's Newsy Bits[1] on my website. New subscribers are offered a free read from another series set in Last Chance Beach.

For MORE Dickens Holiday Romances check out the series page on Amazon, which lists all titles published to date. https://www.amazon.com/dp/B09NX3BQWT The authors of these lovely, holiday themed romances are not done yet. Watch for more Dickens books in 2023!

---

1. https://landing.mailerlite.com/webforms/landing/t6w3o6

Other Romances by Bonnie Edwards

Don't miss out!

Visit the website below and you can sign up to receive emails whenever Bonnie Edwards publishes a new book. There's no charge and no obligation.

https://books2read.com/r/B-A-JXD-WDASB

BOOKS 2 READ

Connecting independent readers to independent writers.

Did you love *The Tinsel Tango A Dickens Holiday Novella*? Then you should read *The Rumball Rumba: A Dickens Holiday Romance*[1] by Bonnie Edwards!

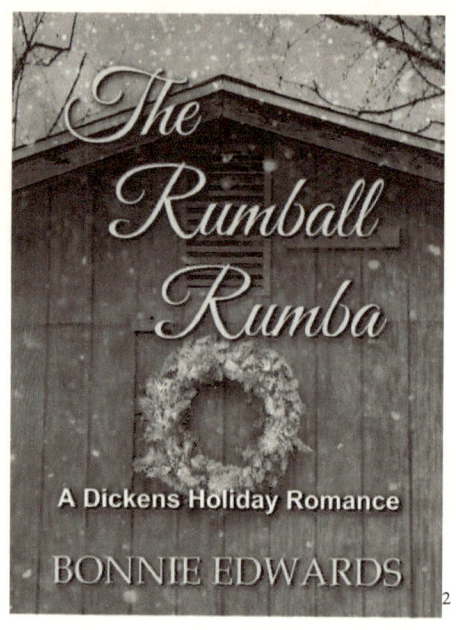

[2]

At Christmas, a secret baby is born in Dickens...Pregnant and divorced, successful artist Trix Warden returns to Dickens to raise her child surrounded by family. To do that, she needs to renovate a horse barn into a gallery/market for other artists.

At 36, her baby is an unexpected miracle that is hers alone. Determined to get everything done before Delivery Day, she hires widowed single father, Jon Carpenter to do her renovations.As they move through the work, they spend time together enjoying the holiday season. Trix helps Jon through tricky times as a parent of teens, and he offers support throughout her pregnancy.Their friendly business

1. https://books2read.com/u/mgEqVK

2. https://books2read.com/u/mgEqVK

relationship blossoms into mutual attraction, and on Christmas Eve, when the baby comes early, Trix trusts Jon with her secret and her heart. But the secret Trix reveals creates a deep divide between them as Jon struggles to accept the decision Trix has made.

Trix is afraid her secret Christmas baby, and her choices, may tear their newfound love to shreds.

Bonus! Includes a recipe for No Bake, No Rum, Rum balls!

Read more at https://www.bonnieedwards.com/.

About the Author

Bonnie Edwards has been writing all her life, starting with a poem about Santa suffering with gout. She was seven, Santa was a thousandteen years old. Delighted with writing, she went on to write family sagas, humorous contemporary romance, romantic suspense and more.

Published by Kensington Books, Harlequin Books, Carina Press, and Robinson (UK) Bonnie's stories stretch from short stories to novellas and novels. Now, she's happy publishing her work herself.

With 40+ titles to her credit, she has been translated into several languages and sold books worldwide. Aside from standalone romances, she has multiple romance series that include Christmas romances and beach reads.

Contemporary family sagas find a home in Return to Welcome. Learn about more exciting releases and get a **free** romance by subscribing to her newsletter, Bonnie's Newsy Bits through her website.

Cheers and happy reading!

Bonnie Edwards

Follow her online: Amazon Website_BookBub_Twitter_Facebook Instagram

Read more at https://www.bonnieedwards.com/.